THE STORY
OF
Peter Pan

THE STORY
OF
Peter Pan

retold from
the fairy play by
Sir James Barrie
by
Daniel O'Connor

Illustrated by
Alice B. Woodward

BELL & HYMAN

First published by G. Bell & Sons Ltd
in October 1907. Reprinted 13 times

Octavo edition first issued November 1914.
Reprinted 38 times

This edition published in 1982 by
Bell & Hyman Limited
Denmark House
37–39 Queen Elizabeth Street
London SE1 2QB

Illustrations © Bell & Hyman Limited

British Library Cataloguing in Publication Data
O'Connor, Daniel
The Story of Peter Pan.
I. Title   II. Barrie, J. M. Peter Pan
823'.912 [J] PZ7

Royalties on sales of this edition of *Peter Pan* go to
the Hospital for Sick Children, Great Ormond Street.

ISBN 0 7135 1351 9

Design and jacket by Malcolm Young
Composition in Garamond by
Filmtype Services Limited, Scarborough, North Yorkshire
Produced in Spain by Grijelmo S.A. Bilbao

Foreword

Sir James Barrie's delightful creation, *Peter Pan*, has by this time taken a secure place in the hearts of children of all ages, and there are few families in the land where Peter, Wendy, Tinker Bell, Captain Hook and the Pirates, the Mermaids and Redskins, and the exciting world in which they lived, are not as well-known as the most time-honoured lore of fairyland.

Mr. Daniel O'Connor's version of the story, issued with Sir James Barrie's kind consent, was the first prose adaptation ever made of the original play. Charmingly illustrated by Alice B. Woodward, it has retained its popularity ever since.

Contents

Illustrations

The Mermaids' Lagoon

The Underground Home

The Pirate Ship

Home, Sweet Home

THE STORY
OF
Peter Pan

Part I

Early Days

In one of the nicest nurseries in the world there were beds for three young people called John Napoleon, and Wendy Moira Angela, and Michael, the children of Mr. and Mrs. Darling. The nursery was wide and airy, with a large window, and a bright fire with a high fire-guard round it, and a big clock, and prettily-coloured nursery-rhyme pictures over the walls. It was in many ways a most interesting household. For one thing, although there was a pretty little parlour-maid called Liza, the children were bathed and dressed by a big dog called Nana, whose kennel was kept in the nursery.

On the evening on which our story begins, Nana was dozing peacefully by the fireside, with her head between her paws. Mr. and Mrs. Darling were getting ready to go out to dinner and Nana was to be left in sole charge of the children. Presently the clock went off with a whirr, and struck – one, two, three, four, five, six – time to begin to put the children to bed.

Nana got up, and stretched herself, and carefully switched on the electric light. You would have been surprised to see how cleverly she managed to do that with her mouth. Then she turned the bedclothes neatly down and hung the little pyjamas over the fire-guard. She then trotted up to the bathroom and turned on the water; after feeling it with her paw to make sure that it was not too hot, she went off to look for Michael, who, being the youngest of the three children, must go to bed first. She returned immediately with him sitting astride on her back as though she were a pony. Michael, of course, did not want to be bathed, but Nana was firm and, taking him to the bathroom, shut the door so that he should not be in a draught. Then Mrs. Darling came to peep at him as he splashed about in the nice warm water.

Whilst Mrs. Darling was in the nursery she

With Michael sitting on her back

heard a noise outside the window, as a tiny figure, no bigger than a little boy, tried the window-latch, and vanished suddenly at her cry of surprise. She flung the window open, but there was nothing to be seen, nothing but the dim roofs of the neighbouring houses, and the deep blue sky above. She began to frighten herself with eerie bogie tales, for the same thing had happened the day before, when Nana had gone to the window and shut it down so quickly that she had cut off the boy's shadow. Mrs. Darling had found it in Nana's mouth, and had carefully folded it and put it away.

But she soon felt reassured when her children came in together in answer to her call. John Napoleon and Wendy were playing at their favourite game of being Father and Mother, and Mrs. Darling's beautiful face beamed with delight as she listened to them. Suddenly, in rushed Mr. Darling, very much excited because he could not fasten his evening tie (evening ties are difficult things to fasten, you know). Mrs. Darling easily managed that for him, and he was soon skipping about the room with Michael on his back, dropping him finally into his bed with a big "bump-ah!"——

Unfortunately, in going to the bathroom, Nana accidently brushed against Mr. Darling's beautifully pressed black trousers, and left some of her grey clinging hairs upon them. Now no grown-up person likes hairy trousers, so Mr. Darling was very cross with Nana, and spoke of dismissing her. But Mrs. Darling told him about the weird apparition at the window, how Nana had barked at it and shut the window down so fast that its shadow had been cut clean off and left behind. She showed him the shadow, and told him how glad she was to have such a treasure as Nana for a nurse. "You see how very useful Nana is," concluded Mrs. Darling, as the faithful dog came in with Michael's bottle of cough mixture. But Michael was naughty, and would not take it; there was a fine fuss over it, when Wendy, being a clever little girl, hit on a brilliant idea.

"Father should take some of *his* medicine to keep Michael company."

"Very well," said Mr. Darling, "we shall see

Mr. Darling only pretended

who is the braver." Two glasses were fetched and filled in a moment. "One, two, three," cried Wendy; Michael took his like a man, but Mr. Darling only pretended to, and quietly hid the glass behind his back. John caught him in the act: "Father hasn't taken his!" he cried, and Michael, seeing that he had been tricked, burst into a loud "Boo-hoo-hoo!" Mr. Darling, to appease Michael, thought of what seemed to him an excellent joke. He poured his medicine into Nana's drinking-bowl, and when poor Nana, thinking that it was something nice, ran eagerly to lap it up, he roared with laughter to see the reproachful eyes she turned upon him. The children, who loved their old nurse very dearly, were terribly distressed as she slunk to her kennel, looking as unhappy and as hurt in her feelings as ever a dog did.

Mr. Darling, angry that they did not enjoy his joke in the least, coaxed Nana out of her kennel, seized her by the collar and dragged her off in disgrace, to be chained up in the yard, "the proper place for dogs," he said, in spite of all their pleading. Mrs. Darling comforted the children, kissing them very tenderly as mothers always do, tucked them up in their beds, sang them to sleep and, leaving the night-lights burning for company, crept softly out of the room to go to the dinner-party with Mr. Darling.

Everything in the big nursery was now still and quiet. Suddenly the night-lights flickered and went out one by one, and there darted into the room a tiny ball of fire, which flitted uneasily about and finally vanished into a jug. Then the same slender graceful figure that had so startled Mrs. Darling leapt from the darkness outside the window. There was just one click, the window was open, and the little creature stepped cautiously in. He seemed to be looking for something; and you will easily guess that what he was looking for was his shadow. "Tink, where are you?" he whispered, and as then the light shone on the jug he went on: "Tink, do you know where they have put it?"

Now this little ball of light was really a fairy girl who knew everything worth knowing. Most fairies do. All you could see of her was the little

Sleep, pretty Darling, do not cry

flame, but you could *hear* her very clearly, she made a tinkling noise like a little silver bell, and that was why she was called Tinker Bell. Tinker Bell at last rested a few moments on the second drawer of the nursery dresser; instantly the boy ran joyfully to it, and pulling open the drawer snatched out his shadow neatly rolled up, just as Mrs. Darling had left it. He had found it certainly, but the next trouble was to put it on again. A happy thought struck him; he would stick it on with soap! Sitting on the hearthrug, he soaped his feet and then he soaped his shadow, but whichever way he soaped they would not stick together. There is no use in having a shadow if it will not stick to you. After trying and trying in vain the poor little fellow gave up the attempt, buried his face in his hands, and sobbed despairingly.

It was then that Wendy awoke. She sat right up in bed, and, not at all frightened, said: "Little boy, why are you crying?"

The elfin creature sprang to his feet, and taking off his cap, bowed very politely. Wendy curtsied in return, though she found it a difficult thing to do in bed.

"What's your name?" asked the little boy.

"Wendy Moira Angela Darling. What's yours?"

"Peter Pan."

"Where do you live?"

"Second turning to the right, and straight on till morning."

This seemed to Wendy a very funny address, but she was all sympathy when she heard that Peter had no mother. No wonder he was crying! But that was not the reason for Peter's tears; he was crying because he could not get his shadow to stick on. This made Wendy smile, and she emphatically declared that soap was no good. It must be sewn on.

"Shall I do it for you?" she suggested, and, jumping out of bed to get her work-basket, she set to work at once. It hurts a good deal to have a shadow sewn on to your feet, but Peter bore it bravely. It was the right thing to do, for the shadow held on beautifully, and Peter was so delighted that he danced up and down the nursery

The shadow held on beautifully

watching it making patterns on the floor as he flung his arms and legs about.

"Oh! the cleverness of me!" cried Peter, overcome with joy, and he crowed with pleasure, for all the world just as a cock would crow.

"You conceited thing," exclaimed Wendy indignantly, "of course *I* did nothing!"

"Oh! you did a little!"

"A little! If I am no use I can at least leave you alone," she said, jumping back into bed and covering her head in a dignified way with the bedclothes.

"Oh! Wendy, please don't leave me alone," Peter exclaimed in great distress. "I can't help crowing when I'm pleased with myself. One girl is more use than twenty boys."

This was rather clever of Peter, and at these sensible words Wendy got up again. She even offered to give Peter a kiss if he liked. Peter looked puzzled, but seeing the thimble on Wendy's finger he thought she meant to give him that, and held out his hand for it. Now Wendy saw at a glance that the poor boy did not even know what a kiss

was, but being a nice little girl of motherly dis-
position, she did not hurt his feelings by laughing
at him, but simply placed the thimble on his
finger.

Peter admired the thimble very much. "Shall I
give you a kiss?" he asked and, jerking a button off
his coat, solemnly presented it to her.

Wendy at once fastened it on a chain which she
wore round her neck, and, forgetting how
muddled he was, she once more asked him for a
kiss.

Immediately he returned the thimble. "Oh!
I didn't mean a *kiss*, I meant a thimble!"

"What's that?" he asked.

"It's like this," replied Wendy, and gently
kissed his cheek.

"Oh!" cried Peter, "how nice!" and he began to
give her *thimbles* in return, and ever afterwards he
called a kiss a thimble, and a thimble a kiss.

"But Peter, how old are you?" continued
Wendy.

"I don't know, but quite young. I ran away the
day I was born."

Wendy gently kissed his cheek

"Ran away – why?"

"Because I heard my father and mother talking about what I was to be when I became a man. I don't want to be a man. I want always to be a little boy and have fun. So I ran away and lived among the fairies."

Wendy was almost speechless with delight at the thought of sitting beside a boy who knew fairies, and after a minute said: "Peter, do you really know fairies?"

"Yes, but they're nearly all dead now. You see, Wendy, when the first baby laughed for the first time, its laugh broke into a thousand pieces, and they all went skipping about, and that was the beginning of fairies. And now, whenever a new baby is born, its first laugh becomes a fairy. So there ought to be a fairy for every little boy and girl, but there isn't. You see children know such a lot now. They soon won't believe in fairies, and whenever a child says: 'I don't believe in fairies,' there's a fairy somewhere that falls down dead."

Peter suddenly looked about the room, as though he were searching for something. Tinker

Bell had disappeared! Before he could grow anxious, however, a tinkling of bells was heard, and Peter, who knew the fairy language, of course understood it. He pulled open the drawer in which his shadow had been hidden, and out sprang Tinker Bell, very angry with him for shutting her up accidentally in the drawer. She skipped about the room, but Wendy gave such a cry of delight that Tink was frightened and hid behind the clock.

"But Peter," continued Wendy, "if you don't live with the fairies, where do you live?"

"I live with the Lost Boys."

"Who are they?"

"Why, they are the children who fall out of their prams when their nurses are looking the other way. If they are not claimed within seven days, they are sent far away to the Never-Never-Never Land. I'm their Captain."

"Oh! what fun! But, Peter, why did you come to our nursery window?"

Peter told her that he came to listen to the lovely stories Wendy's mother told her children, for the

Lost Boys had no mothers, and no one to tell them any stories. He also told her how he led them against their enemies, the pirates and the wolves, and how they enjoyed bathing in the Lagoon, where beautiful mermaids sang and swam all day long.

"I must go back now," he went on, "the boys will be anxious to hear the end of the story about the Prince and the Glass Slipper. I told them as much as I knew, and they're longing to hear the rest."

Wendy begged him to stay.

"I'll tell you lots more," she promised, "ever so many stories if you'll only stay."

"Come with me, Wendy!" exclaimed Peter, struck with a new idea. "You can tell us all the stories there, and darn our clothes, and tuck us in at night. None of us has ever been tucked in. All the boys long for a mother. Oh, Wendy, do come!"

It was a tempting idea to Wendy, but a sudden thought came across her mind. "Peter, I can't! Think of Mummy! Besides, I can't fly."

"I'll teach you, Wendy."

This was too much for her. "Peter, will you teach John and Michael to fly as well?"

"Yes, if you like."

So John and Michael were awakened, and directly they heard that there were pirates in the Never-Never-Never Land they began to clamour to go at once. They watched Peter fly about the room, and tried to imitate him, flapping their arms clumsily at first like baby birds, and flopping about all over the place.

"That will never do," Peter said, "I must blow the fairy dust on you. Now waggle your shoulders as I do."

So they tried, and found that they could fly; just a little at first, from the bed to the floor and back again; then over the bed and across the room, and then, as they grew braver, almost as freely and easily as Peter himself.

"Tink, lead the way!" called Peter, and the fairy shot out like a little star. None of the children had time to put on their day clothes, but John snatched his top hat as he flew out of the window, followed

Away they floated

by Michael. Peter Pan held Wendy's hand, and away they floated into the dark blue depths of the starry night.

A minute afterwards Mrs. Darling, who had just returned from the party, rushed into the nursery with Nana at her heels, for Nana had been anxious about her charges, and had just succeeded in breaking her chain. But it was too late. The children were already on their way to the Never-Never-Never Land.

Part II

The Never-Never-Never Land

Far away in the Never-Never-Never Land the
Lost Boys lived in the depths of the forest, on
the banks of a lake now covered with ice. The trees
were bare without their summer dress, and wolves
prowled and howled in the distance, and wild
beasts snarled in the undergrowth, and Pirates
sailed villainously up the lake, and Red Indians,
who were friends of the boys, lived secretly in
their wigwams hidden in the glades of the woods.

The Lost Boys, who, in their fur coats, looked
more like bears than boys, were anxiously await-
ing Peter's return. There were six of them: Slightly
Soiled, the eldest; then came Tootles, and Nibs,
and Curly, and the Twins, who were so much
alike that one name did for both of them, so each
was called Twin. They lived like moles under the

45

ground, for fear of the Pirates and the wolves.
Each one had a special staircase hollowed in a tree-
trunk, so that they could easily run down among
the roots of the trees into their home. They were
playing about happily, although they were beginning to be a little anxious that Peter was so long
away. Slightly was tootling on a whistle, and
dancing quite merrily, with an ostrich for partner
(an odd companion, you will say), when suddenly
the gruff voices of the Pirates were heard. Nibs,
who was very brave, slipped away through the
trees to scout, but the others had only just time to
scuttle down the stairs in the hollow trees before
the big ugly buccaneers came tramping up, haul-
ing their captain, who was sitting in state upon a
sledge.

You could not imagine a more dreadful-looking
villain than that man was. His name was James
Hook, and it suited him! He had two most evil-
looking black eyes, his face was seamed with lines
which seemed to express his wicked thoughts, his
hideous chin, all unshaven, was as black as ink and
as prickly as a furze-bush, his hair was long and

There were six of them

Slightly was dancing with an ostrich

black, and it hung around his face in greasy curls. He was singing a horrible song about himself, keeping time by swinging in the air the gruesome stump of his right arm. At the end of it a double iron-pronged hook was fixed instead of a hand. That was how he got his name. That man was the most wicked pirate who ever lived! He simply wallowed in wickedness! Even his own crew were terrified of him; and they were as bad as could be! So no wonder the Lost Boys darted like rabbits to their cave.

Now Captain Hook most of all wanted to find Peter Pan, for it was Peter who, a long time before, in a battle between the Pirates and the Lost Boys, had cut off his right arm and flung it to a passing crocodile. The crocodile had liked the taste of it so much that ever since he had wandered from land to land and from sea to sea licking his lips for the rest of the Captain.

The Captain had naturally some reason for hating Peter, for he had a dreadful time in escaping from the greedy crocodile, but still the beast dogged his footsteps, and followed him on and on and on by land and sea wherever he went. The Captain only got a start when the crocodile was asleep, and with that and a swift ship he had managed so far to escape. It was an awful life!

Fortunately for Hook, the crocodile had once, in an ill-advised moment, swallowed an alarm clock (one of those patent ninety-nine-years clocks, guaranteed to go any time, anywhere and anyhow). Go it did, and it ticked so loudly that the Captain could always hear it coming, and it was the signal for him to bolt!

Hook sat down on one of the enormous forest mushrooms (in the Never-Never-Never Land mushrooms grow to a gigantic size) to think how to get his revenge. He was in the middle of a torrent of braggings and boastings when he felt his seat getting not only warm, but much too warm. And it was little wonder! For when he furiously leapt up he found that he had really been sitting on a chimney of the underground home which Peter had cleverly disguised. He realised at once that the Lost Boys must be living in safety down below.

Very soon he had a wicked, treacherous plan

"The Crocodile! The Crocodile!"

settled. He determined to cook a huge rich cake, with beautiful green icing and a poisoned inside. He was sure that the Lost Boys, who had no mother to look after them, would eat it greedily, and die with awful pains inside. Smee, as the Captain's wily lieutenant was called, was overjoyed at this plan, and chuckled loudly.

"Shake hands on't," said Hook, but Smee did not want to, and begged to be excused.

"Paw, Smee, paw," said the Captain in an awful voice, so Smee had to take the horrid hook in his hand, and they both danced round while Hook sang with diabolical grimaces:

> *"Yo ho, yo ho, when I say 'Paw'*
> *By fear they're overtook;*
> *Naught's left upon your bones when you*
> *Have shaken hands with Hook."*

Just as he was gloating over his pleasant scheme a queer sound was heard, like a corncrake coming nearer and nearer through a barley field. "Tick, tack, tick, tack, tick, tack."

"The Crocodile! the Crocodile!" the Pirate

Captain yelled, and in a moment was flying for his life.

The Pirates had scarcely disappeared in the depths of the forest when the Indians crept silently up in pursuit of them. Tiger Lily, their chieftainess, was at their head, now running swiftly under the trees, now listening with her ear to the ground, to know where her enemies had gone. For, like Tinker Bell and Wendy, she loved Peter Pan, and his enemies were her enemies.

The Redskins slid along, following the Pirates with steps as quiet as those of a beetle crawling through the grass. They soon passed far out of sight, and then, one by one, the Lost Boys peeped from their tree-trunks and, seeing that all was quiet, came out again to their playground in the woods.

But their safety did not last for long. A fierce barking of wolves was heard, and Nibs, who had gone off by himself, rushed, quite out of breath, into the midst of the Boys, closely pursued by a pack of lean and hungry wolves with glittering fiery eyes. What were the Lost Boys to do in this

The Indians crept silently up

terrible plight, when their leader was far away? Fortunately, one of them remembered Peter's plan. Whenever he was attacked by wild beasts Peter used to run at them backwards, jumping along the ground, squinting at them through his legs. The Lost Boys did this all together, and really, it was so astonishing that the wolves fled with terrified howls to the thickets where they lived.*

Then Nibs told the Boys how he had seen the loveliest white bird you could imagine.

"It was flying this way," he said, "it looked so wearied, and as it flew it moaned 'Poor Wendy'."

"Are you sure it was a bird?" they asked.

Nibs was quite sure, and almost at once they saw Wendy flying through the trees in her white night-gown. Tinker Bell was by her side, darting at her, and telling the Boys that Peter wanted her shot, for Tinker was rather a bad little fairy sometimes. She said this because she was jealous of Wendy, since Peter and Wendy had kissed each other.

*This is a good way of scaring away mad bulls and wild animals, but it is always safer to practise on cows or in the Zoo *first*.

Instantly, Tootles seized his bow and arrow, and shot at the bird, as he thought, and Wendy fell fainting to the ground.

At once the Boys saw that she was no bird, but a little girl, and perhaps the very mother whom Peter had promised to bring them. They were very frightened, and soon were sure that they had done a dreadful thing, for Peter came flying down with John and Michael, and immediately asked after Wendy.

"She flew this way, haven't you seen her?" he asked.

"Yes," said Tootles, and pointed to her as she lay motionless on the ground.

Peter bent over her and took the arrow, and, in his anger, would have killed Tootles with it, if Wendy had not stopped him by feebly moving her hand. Then they were all glad, for Wendy was not dead, as they had thought, but only stunned. The arrow had fortunately struck the button which Peter had given her in mistake for a kiss. Soon she was quite well again, but faint and tired after her long flight through the air.

She lay motionless on the ground

The Boys did not know what to do. They did not like to carry her down into the cave, as it might not be sufficiently respectful, so they planned to build a house over her. Only they did not know what kind of house to build.

Then Wendy sang in her half-sleep the kind of house she wanted:

> *"I wish I had a darling house,*
> *The littlest ever seen.*
> *With funny little red walls,*
> *And roof of mossy green."*

and the Boys fetched logs out of the forest, and a grate and a rug from the underground cave, and built a beautiful home for her out of wood, and tarpaulin, and make-believe. They made a chimney out of John's tall hat, which he had been Londony enough to bring with him, and they made a splendid knocker out of the sole of one of Tootles' boots.

When it was finished – it was built round Wendy as she lay on the ground – Peter knocked solemnly at the door, and Wendy opened it and came out, very pleased and happy. The Lost Boys knelt before her, and begged her to be their Mother, and tuck them in at night-time, and tell them stories before they went to bed. She said that she was not quite sure if she could, but she would do her best, if only Peter would be Father, and that now, if they liked to come in, she would tell them the story of Cinderella.

In they bundled, one after the other, to listen to the tale. And they were so big, and the house was so small, that they must have been packed like sardines inside. But a sort of cosy feeling like that was, I expect, just what they wanted, and they were very happy.

The evening fell softly down on the forest, and the shadows rose, so that everything was dark and still, except for the occasional baying of a wolf. Lights were lit in the little house, and at last, when it was quite night, Peter came out with his sword, and walked up and down like a sentry, to guard the new little mother he had brought for the Lost Boys.

The Lost Boys knelt before her

Part III

The Mermaids' Lagoon

One fine summer evening Peter, with Wendy and their little family, went down to the Lagoon where the Mermaids lived. The Never-Never-Never Land, as you see, is full of the most strange and interesting creatures; some of them dreadful, like the Pirates, wolves, and crocodiles; others, like the fairies and the mermaids, altogether beautiful and charming. Wendy and her brothers, who had never seen a real mermaid with a tail, were very much excited, and, as luck would have it, just as they arrived at the lagoon, one of them, seated on a rock, was combing her long tresses, on which the sunlight gleamed, until they shone like a mixture of gold and bronze, for they had a beautiful greenish tinge. As she combed her hair she sang such a wonderful melody that the boys longed to catch her. They instantly dashed into the water, but with a piercing cry of "Mortals!" the Mermaid dived out of their reach into the lowest depths.

"But look! here is another little mermaid! Surely we can catch her!" said John Napoleon Darling, and he very nearly did. Mermaids, however, are hard to catch, and when caught, are still harder to hold. John succeeded in getting the little sprite in his hands but, wriggling like an eel, she slipped out of his grasp. Breathless with excitement, the whole band of children clambered on to the rocks, when all at once a cry went up: "The Pirates!" Sure enough a boat was approaching, and in it were seated the two pirate lieutenants, Smee and Starkey. The boys were already swimming to the shore as fast as they could, when to his horror Peter recognised Tiger Lily sitting in the stern, tightly bound with ropes. In a flash he guessed what their plan was. The wretches meant to leave her, all bound as she was, upon the rock, until the tide came up and drowned her.

Determined to save her, Peter thought of a

She was combing her long tresses

She slipped out of his grasp

Tiger Lily was tightly bound with ropes

clever trick. Imitating the wicked Captain's voice he called out: "Cut her bonds and let her go!" The effect was marvellous: the astonished buccaneers, fearing to disobey their Captain, instantly released Tiger Lily, who leapt into the water and swam towards the boys.

The Pirates had turned and were rowing back, when they saw Hook swimming towards them. Horribly enraged, he chased them out of the boat, leaving them to swim back to the ship as best they might, while he himself set about recapturing Tiger Lily.

But once the Pirates were safely out of the way, Peter and his friends went back to the rock to attack the Captain, who was now single-handed. A fierce fight followed, Hook using his iron prong to slash at poor Peter, while the boys, seizing Hook's boat, rowed off with Tiger Lily in it. At last, finding himself outdone, the Captain gave up the fight, and in all haste swam back to his ship.

Peter, left alone on the rock with Wendy, found her so exhausted that she could neither swim nor fly any farther. With difficulty he managed to help her to a firm footing, but the tide was rising, and they were both in great danger. As he watched the water silently creeping nearer, Peter almost despaired. But all at once a large kite came flying slowly over the lagoon. In a second Peter had seized its tail, and binding it tightly round Wendy, he sent her sailing away in safety, bravely calling "Good-bye Wendy!" until she was out of sight.

Then indeed, as the tide rose steadily, Peter was in great danger. The water reached his feet, and he was beginning to think it would be a "tremendous adventure to die," when who should come sailing by but a great sea-bird on its nest, which had been blown off the cliffs by the rising storm. "Hurrah!" cried Peter, "there's a lovely boat for me!" and chasing the bird off, in he stepped, curled himself round and, spreading out his coat to the wind, sailed swiftly and merrily after Wendy.

A fierce fight followed

Spreading his coat to the wind

Part IV

The Underground Home

The days passed happily in the underground home, where Wendy was the sweetest little mother, and Peter the bravest father you could ever have found anywhere. The cave was large and roomy, and the rocks out of which it was hollowed were of a deep brown colour. There was a fine large fireplace, and overhead, near the ceiling, were hung baskets and fishing-tackle and all sorts of things likely to be useful to cave-dwellers.

Wendy had not been there long before she had improved the home and made it as comfortable as her own nursery. It is wonderful what clever girls can do, even with the poorest materials. There was now a huge bed for all the Boys, and a basket for Michael, because he was the littlest and because a cradle is such a homely thing to have about the house. And in a corner of the room, hidden behind a tiny crimson curtain, there was a little room for Tinker Bell, daintily furnished to suit the tastes of a girl fairy. There were stools made of mushrooms for the Boys, and two comfortable chairs made of pumpkins, where Peter and Wendy could sit in state, as was fitting for the father and mother of the little family.

One Saturday night, Wendy and the Boys were all downstairs together, waiting for Peter to come back from a hunting expedition. Outside, the faithful Tiger Lily and her Red Indian band were keeping guard against the Pirates.

Presently the crackling of branches signalled Peter's approach through the undergrowth. Tiger Lily sprang up to meet him, and the Lost Boys ran to the tree-trunk stairways to welcome him on his return. He was the best of fathers. He never forgot to fill his pockets with fruit for the boys who had been good, and he let them rummage through and through his coat like rats in a corn sack.

Then he turned towards Wendy, who was very busy mending the children's socks by the fireside.

Wendy told her story

She looked very charming in her pretty brown frock the colour of autumn leaves, with scarlet berries in her hair, and she made Peter very happy as they exchanged thimbles and talked over the boys and their doings as if they had really been their father and mother. When the children clamoured for a dance, Peter even said that he was too old for such a game, and that his old bones would simply rattle, and Wendy also thought that the mother of such an armful could not go skipping about with her children. So Peter sang "Sally in our Alley," which Wendy thought no one else in all the world could sing so sweetly as the darling of her heart, while the others danced pillow dances, and bolster dances, and turned somersaults on the beds, and did all the other jolly and lively things that everyone wants to do just about bedtime, when one ought to be thinking of going to sleep.

At last they quietened down for Wendy to tell them just one more story before they were tucked in for the night. They clustered eagerly round, interrupting every sentence, as children always do, even the best of them, while Wendy told her story. And the story somehow seemed familiar to John, and Michael, and Peter, for it was the tale of Mr. and Mrs. Darling, poor dears, who had lost their children one winter night; and how sad they were about it, how lonely they felt, and how the nursery window would always be kept open, ready for the children, if ever they should come flying home again.

When she had finished, Peter stood up sadly. "No, Wendy," he said, "I thought so once, but you cannot be sure that the window will be kept open. When I went back to my mother, the window was barred, and there was another little boy sleeping in my cradle." At that thought, Wendy started up with a look of horror in her face: "Perhaps by this time, Mother may be starting to forget us," she exclaimed, and John and Michael felt they dared not stay another moment in the Never-Never-Never Land.

What would they do if they were too late in coming back, and found other children in their beds, other children being bathed and dressed by

Seized by one of the swarthy ruffians

Nana? They must go home at once.

The Boys crowded round Wendy, begging her not to leave them, but she was firm. Not only would she return with John and Michael, but she would take all the Boys with her, for her mother to adopt. The Boys, as soon as they heard themselves invited to come too, were as happy as larks. For now each of them would have a true mother in Mrs. Darling, and would live in a house like other boys. In a moment they were packing their baby clothes, and were ready to start on their journey.

Peter alone refused. He was miserable at the thought of losing Wendy, but he couldn't agree to grow old and have a beard, as he knew he must do if he left the Never-Never-Never Land. Never, never, could he do that! There was nothing for him, then, but to stay behind. Wendy was as careful as a little mother in pouring out Peter's medicine, and made him promise faithfully to take it every night.

But suddenly there was a stamping overhead, and a banging and a clashing, and a shouting, and a sound of heavy people wrestling and struggling to and fro. The Pirates had taken the Red Indians by surprise. The children heard the fighting, and listened like mice to the squalling of cats, as frightened as could be, while Peter waited with his sword. The battle was very soon over. The Redskins were beaten and ran like hares, or crawled dangerously wounded into the thickets. The triumphant Pirates were left victorious, though a little out of breath, close above the children's heads.

Hook, their captain, more wicked-looking than ever, listened at the mushroom chimney. "If the Indians have won," Peter was saying, "they'll beat the tom-tom."

"Aha!" thought Hook, and he picked up a tom-tom that one of the flying Indians had left behind, and sounded it loudly; "rub-a-dub, rub-a-dub, dub, dub, dub."

"Hurrah!" shouted the children down below. "An Indian victory!"

"All will be safe," said Peter. "You may go now! Tink will show you the way," and bidding

Transported to the pirate ship

a hurried good-bye to Peter, away they all went up the stairways in the tree-trunks, out into the forest.

The Pirates were ready for them. As each child came above the ground, he was seized by one of the swarthy ruffians who stood waiting. One by one, and silently, they were captured and flung into boats and carried to the pirate ship, which had anchored in the lake close by.

Everything had been done so quietly that Peter was quite unaware of his friends' sad fate. He only knew that he was all alone, that Wendy had left him, and that she, and Michael, and John, and all the Lost Boys who had been his companions were on their way from the Never-Never-Never Land to the country of the ordinary people who wear city clothes as soon as they are old enough, and grow up one after the other. Poor Peter threw himself on his bed and sobbed himself to sleep.

Hook was still lurking about, for the thing that annoyed him most was that Peter had not left the cave with the rest, and was still safe.

But in his wicked heart a wicked scheme had

already risen by which he hoped to kill his enemy. He had carefully listened to Wendy's last words: "Be sure and take your medicine, Peter." Here was the Captain's last chance. Creeping down to the door of the cave, he stretched his long arm round the ledge just inside, and poured a few drops of deadly poison into the glass, and, with a grin of triumph on his ugly face, he threw his cloak over his shoulder and stole away.

"Tap, tap, tap." Somebody was knocking at the door. "Who's there?" asked Peter sleepily.

"Tap, tap, tap."

He got up and opened the door. Tinker Bell, tinkling excitedly, flew into the room. "The Pirates have captured them!" she tinkled, "the Pirates have captured them!" As Peter excitedly snatched up his sword and sharpened it very sharply on the grindstone, he remembered his medicine. He reached for it, but before he could take it, Tinker Bell flew into it and drank it all up. He soon learnt the reason, when his little fairy told him, in a weak voice, that it was poisoned, and that she had drunk the poison as the only way to

Tinker Bell flew into his glass

save his life. It was indeed an act of self-sacrifice; for Tink knew only too well how much Peter loved Wendy, and that no warning of hers would prevent him from keeping his promise.

Poor Tinker Bell was dying. Peter, in a frenzy of grief and with tears in his eyes, made this passionate appeal to all children: "Do you believe in fairies? If you do, clap your hands, and that will save poor Tinker Bell." As his cry rang round the world, there came an echo of sound as of millions of little hands clapping, as if all the children throughout the world knew suddenly that of course they believed in fairies.

The result was magical. Tinker Bell was saved; her light, which had been getting fainter and fainter, grew brighter and brighter again; the merry sound of tinkling (her way of speaking to Peter) which had almost faded away, now grew stronger and stronger. She was once more the bright little fairy that went with Peter to the Darling nursery, and again, under her guidance, Peter set out to rescue the Boys and Wendy.

Part V

The Pirate Ship

The pirate ship was a terribly evil-looking craft with its painted sails, its heavy tarred ropes, and its flag with the skull and crossbones upon it, flapping grimly at the stern. The poor children were at once driven into the dark and dirty hold, while Hook walked the deck, rubbing his hands and chuckling to himself to think that at last he had them in his power.

"Are all the prisoners chained so that they can't fly away?" he asked Smee, who was very busy at his sewing-machine.

"Aye, aye, Captain," answered Smee.

"Then hoist them up," shouted the Captain.

He seated himself on a chair covered with a white bearskin, waiting while the Boys, whose wrists were chained together, were dragged out of the hold and brought before him. Six of them, he said, were to walk the plank at once, but he would save any two who were willing to be cabin boys. The children were not at first sure what walking the plank meant, but Hook soon showed them by roaring out a song in explanation.

> *"Yo ho! yo ho! the frisky plank,*
> *You walk along it so –*
> *Till it goes down and you goes down*
> *To too-ral loo-ral lo –"*

he sang, waving his hook to show how, when the plank tipped, they would be shot into the water and drowned.

Turning towards John Napoleon Darling he shouted: "You look as if you had some pluck in you!" John hesitated. In his schoolboy days he had always thought a pirate's life very attractive, so stepping forward, he said: "Will you call me Red-handed Jack?" The Captain laughed with delight, and promised to give him that name if he joined the crew. Then Michael went up to him and slapped him on the shoulder. "What will you call

The pirate ship

me if I join?" he asked. "Black-Bearded Joe," answered the Captain, and Michael was very pleased. But then the cabin boys were told that they must of course swear "Down with the King!" and to this neither boy would consent. John and Michael were pushed on one side and told that their fate was sealed, while Hook shouted, "Bring up their mother."

In a moment Wendy was dragged from the hold, and when the Boys rushed to protect her they were pulled back, leaving her standing alone, looking very frightened but pretty in her brown dress, with a long brown cloak wrapped round her. Hook asked her if she had any last message for her sons who were about to die. Wendy spoke beautifully to the Boys, telling them she was sure their real mothers would wish them to die like English gentlemen. Her courage so inspired the children that they all cried they would do what their mothers wished. Upon this, Wendy was cruelly tied to the mast whilst Hook's orders were being carried out.

But, just as the Boys' fate seemed determined,

something happened to change Hook's glee into terror. "Tick! tick! ter-ick, tick, tick!" he heard, and at the dreaded sound he yelled: "The crocodile! hide me, hide me!" In abject fear he rushed to a corner of the ship while his men crowded round him, intent only upon shielding their captain from the jaws of the monster. The Boys, too, waited breathless with horror, until with sudden relief and rapture they saw not the crocodile but their beloved captain Peter Pan appearing over the ship's side. In one hand, at arm's length, he held an alarm clock, which had made Hook believe that the crocodile was upon him.

Making a sign to his friends, Peter dashed into the cabin, unseen by the Pirates, and shut the door. The ticking ceased at once and Hook's terror vanished.

Returning to his dreadful purpose he cried: "Now here's to Johnny Plank!" Again he began to sing, "Yo ho, yo ho, the frisky plank," but the Boys, filled with hope and excitement, drowned his voice by singing "Rule, Britannia," and just as the Pirate was about to vent his rage upon them he

"That man is mine!"

was silenced by a shrill and piercing cock's-crow from the cabin.

Struck motionless with terror, the crew looked to their Captain for some explanation. He ordered Gecco, one of his men, to enter the cabin and see what was the matter. Hook waited, but Gecco did not return, and once again was heard the awful mysterious crowing. Hook sent in another of his men, but he did not come back either. "Someone must bring me out that doodle-doo," roared the Captain, and, as no one volunteered, "I thought I heard Starkey volunteer," he said, pointing his hook at Starkey. Mad with terror of the hook as well as of the uncanny creature in the cabin, Starkey rushed wildly round the deck, and finally, to escape both, flung himself overboard.

Furious at this mutinous behaviour, Hook shouted, "I'll bring that doodledoo out myself," but he had no better success, and came rushing back in a cowardly fashion, saying: "Something blew out the light."

A happy idea now struck him. "Drive the Boys

in – let them fight the doodledoo – if they kill him so much the better, if he kills them we're none the worse.''

This, of course, was just what the children wanted, but, concealing their delight, they allowed themselves to be driven into the cabin. In the meantime, all the Pirates huddled together, hiding their faces. Sailors, you know, are very superstitious, and they all thought the ship was bewitched. So terrified were they that no one saw Peter steal out, followed by the Boys, who crept silently up the ladder to the higher deck. No one saw Peter cut the ropes which bound Wendy, and take her place at the mast, and cover his face with the brown cloak she had left, while Wendy joined the Boys.

''It's the girl!'' cried Hook, ''there's never luck on a pirate ship with a woman aboard; let's throw her over.'' All the men knew that their Captain was right, and one of the Pirates started up and shook his fist at the brown-robed figure at the mast. ''There's nothing can save you now, Missy,'' he cried. ''There is one,'' came a ringing

Right into the jaws of the crocodile!

voice, and the brown cloak was flung aside and there stood Peter Pan. "Down, Boys, and at them," he shouted, and with a rush the Boys, armed with weapons which Peter had found and given them in the cabin, swarmed down upon the lower deck. The Pirates believed that all the Boys had been slain by the mysterious doodledoo, and were panic-stricken as they saw them with swords and daggers. Some of the crew rushed to the bulwarks and leapt overboard; others with their knives fell upon the Boys, while Hook backed into the cabin fighting for his life. "Put up your knives, Boys, that man is mine!" cried Peter, pointing to Hook. The Boys turned their attention to the rest of the pirate crew, who were one by one forced into the sea, while the two mortal enemies appeared at the cabin door closed in deadly combat. Each was determined to kill the other. Their swords clashed and step by step Hook was driven back to the side of the ship. He felt himself weakening. In despair he cried out:

"'Tis some terrible fiend fighting me! Who are you, Pan?"

"I'm youth!" cried Peter, "I'm joy! I'm youth!"

With that he wrenched Hook's sword from him and pushed him into the sea, right into the jaws of the waiting crocodile, who caught him and ate him up at last.

The Boys burst into ringing cheers as they and Wendy crowded round their leader, who stood like a conquering hero while the pirate flag was lowered.

All the pirates save two, Smee and Starkey, jumped into the sea and were drowned.

Smee, the Irish Pirate, who was not so wicked as the rest of the crew, managed to swim ashore, and later became a reformed character and a brave sailor in His Majesty's Fleet.

Starkey, who had never shed blood, but had been guilty of many cruel deeds, was captured by the Redskins and led a miserable life, for Great Big Little White Panther, the Indian chief, forced him to act as nurse to the papooses of the tribe – a sad come-down for a wicked pirate!

Nurse to the papooses!

Part VI

Home, Sweet Home

But at home in the Darling household all this time there was deep sorrow. Mr. Darling, as a punishment to himself for taking their guardian Nana away, had vowed that he would live in the kennel till his children's return. For months now he had lived in it, and had been carried to business in it every morning, much to the disgust of the prim little housemaid Liza. Mr. Darling had become quite a celebrity, and great ladies, leaders of society, found him so interesting and touching, that they all cried out as he passed by, "Oh, do come to dinner at our house, do come in the kennel!" All the newspapers had asked him to write the cricket and football news for them, and his picture postcards were to be seen in every shop window.

But it happened one evening, when he returned from business, carried as usual in the kennel, he was taken up to the now deserted nursery, where Mrs. Darling spent most of her time mourning for her lost children, while the faithful Nana tried in vain to cheer her up. "George, George, I believe you are beginning to *like* that kennel," she said reproachfully, as he crawled out. He denied the charge, however, and tried to comfort Mrs. Darling, who never for one moment forgot the little empty beds and the silence and cheerlessness of the nursery. Then he left her, and sitting down by the fire, Mrs. Darling was alone with her sad thoughts.

Scarcely, however, had she closed her eyes when three little figures flew in at the window and nestled cosily in their beds. Then softly Wendy called to her mother. But when Mrs. Darling looked round she simply couldn't believe that the children were really there. So many times before she had dreamt of their return, that it was not till they all three crowded round her that she realised that they had indeed come home. Oh! what joy to

He would live in the kennel

Those dear faces pressed against hers

feel once more those dear faces, cool and fresh from the flight through the night air, pressed against hers, hot with tears; to hear once more the sound of those sweet voices as they all talked at once. At last, when she was a little calm, Wendy began telling her about Peter Pan and the Lost Boys, who with Peter Pan himself were all waiting outside. Directly Mrs. Darling saw them, and heard that they had no mothers, she instantly adopted them all. Though the house would be rather crowded, she could easily put up extra beds in the drawing-room, she said, and all could be comfortably managed.

The only difficulty lay with Peter. Much as at first sight he loved Mrs. Darling, much as he loved Wendy, he couldn't agree to grow up. So at last it was arranged that he should fly back alone to the Never-Never-Never Land, and that once a year Mrs. Darling would allow Wendy to go and stay with him for a whole week to do his spring cleaning.

THE TREE TOPS

High in the tree tops of the Never-Never-Never Land, Tinker Bell placed the little house that was built for Wendy. The tree tops are soft as velvet, and in the evening at twilight are all bejewelled with tiny mauve, and white, and blue lights. The mauve ones are boy fairies, the white, girl fairies, and the blue lights are darling little sillies who are not quite sure what they are.

And the still air is filled with the singing of birds and the ringing of hundreds of little fairy bells. But the sweetest sound of all is the fluting of Peter Pan's pipe as he sits outside the little house and calls to the spring to make haste, because with the spring comes Wendy.

With the spring comes Wendy